Ocean Wide, Ocean Deep

by SUSAN LENDROTH

Illustrations by RAÚL ALLÉN

TRICYCLE PRESS
Berkeley/Toronto

*O*h, ocean wide, ocean deep,
will you rock Papa to sleep?
He sailed tonight on the evening tide—
please keep him safe, oh, ocean wide.

*C*ome morning I arise at dawn,
to ask again how long he's gone.
Mama braids my hair and ties a bow,
then answers with her voice pitched low,

"Probably a year or more.
They're sailing to a foreign shore
to bring home lacquer, tea, and jade.
Your father's joined the China trade."

Mama hands me the porridge ladle
then lifts the baby from his cradle,
"Breakfast first, then off to school,
and take your shawl—the morning's cool."

The winds blow cold for early May,
pushing whitecaps 'cross the bay.
I watch birds pull worms from the grass
and think how slowly seasons pass.

*B*y August Baby has learned to stand,
toes curling in the warm, bright sand.
I bring him to our favorite beach
where green crabs scuttle out of reach.

Within a pocket of bubbling foam,
I find a snail's abandoned home—
its empty corridors curled up tight
in polished swirls of milky white.

I hold the seashell to my ear
then whisper words only seagulls hear,
"Remind Papa to think of me,"
and throw the shell back out to sea.

*A*s autumn flings her fiery cloak
over the sumac, beech, and oak,
I dream of silks in every hue
and willowware of deepest blue. . .

. . . moss–green jade and darkest teak,
all the treasures traders seek.

With Papa I'd browse those crowded shops
where merchants seal their deals with chops.

*A*gainst December's frozen blast
we bar the doors and shutters fast.
But still I hear the raging waves
and wonder what storms Papa braves.

From the nest of quilts upon my bed,
I tell Mama of my growing dread
that somewhere in a howling gale
my father battles sleet and hail . . .

. . . or between Sumatra and the Cape
he's met pirates he can't escape.

"If I could soar just like the gulls,
I'd swoop down on those pirate hulls.
Why can't sailors bring their daughters
to stand by them in distant waters?"

Mama takes my hand and clasps it tight—
her lullaby holds back the night.

*S*pring returns and greens the trees,
then summer warms the ocean breeze.
My little brother's begun to talk,
a happy babbling while we walk.

*O*ne afternoon it's growing late
when I spy a familiar gait;
a tall man's striding up our lane,
whistling a well-known refrain.

"Papa!" I scream as I race

   full tilt into his warm embrace.

   He lifts me high into the air;

   I smell the sea laced through his hair.

   Mama runs to us but doesn't speak;

   tears slide slowly down her cheek.

*A*fter supper Papa spins fine tales,
of ports and spices, ships and whales.

*O*h, ocean wide, ocean deep,
hush, my family's gone to sleep.
Our Papa's tucked up snug inside—
you kept him safe,

oh, ocean wide.

For my mother and father, who sang me to sleep. —S.L.
For Luis. —R.A.

GLOSSARY

China trade: during the 1800s, many ships sailed to China from America and Europe to bring back luxury goods such as porcelain, jade, and tea. Voyages could last a year or longer and families often received no word from loved ones at sea until the ships returned to port.

Chops: official carved seals or stamps. Merchants pressed the chops in ink and stamped documents with them.

Teak: a valuable wood, much prized for furniture.

Willowware: blue and white porcelain painted with scenes of willow trees, pagodas, etc. The pattern is still popular today.

The author wishes to thank Professor Dane A. Morrison of Salem State College for his kind assistance, and her editor, Abigail Samoun, for her belief in this project.

TRICYCLE PRESS
an imprint of Ten Speed Press
PO Box 7123
Berkeley, California 94707
www.tricyclepress.com

Design by Susan Van Horn
Typeset in Pelican and Bembo
The illustrations in this book were rendered in pencil and watercolor, and finished digitally using Photoshop.

Library of Congress Cataloging-in-Publication Data

Lendroth, Susan.
Ocean wide, ocean deep / by Susan Lendroth ; illustrated by Raúl Allén.
p. cm.
Summary: In nineteenth-century New England, a young girl watches her baby brother learn to walk and talk while waiting for Papa's return from the sea after he joins the China trade and sails to foreign lands.
ISBN 978-1-58246-232-5
[1. Family life—New England—Fiction. 2. Sailors—Fiction. 3. New England—History—19th century—Fiction. 4. Stories in rhyme.] I. Allén, Raúl, ill. II. Title.
PZ8.3.L5397Oce 2007
[E]—dc22
2007018619

First Tricycle Press printing, 2008
Printed in China.

1 2 3 4 5 6 — 12 11 10 09 08